MARY, MARY, QUITE CONTRARY

Mary, Mary, quite contrary,
How does your garden grow?
With silver bells and cockle shells
And pretty maids all in a row.

SING A SONG OF SIXPENCE

Sing a song of sixpence,
A pocket full of rye;
Four-and-twenty blackbirds
Baked in a pie.

When the pie was opened,
The birds began to sing;
Wasn't that a dainty dish
To set before the king?

The king was in his counting house,
Counting out his money;
The queen was in the parlor,
Eating bread and honey.

The maid was in the garden,
Hanging out the clothes,
When down came a blackbird
And snapped off her nose.

SULKY SUE

Here's Sulky Sue, what shall we do?
Turn her face to the wall till she comes to.

PETER, PETER, PUMPKIN EATER

Peter, Peter, pumpkin eater,
Had a wife and couldn't keep her;
He put her in a pumpkin shell,
And there he kept her very well.

LITTLE MISS MUFFIT

Little Miss Muffit sat on a tuffet,
Eating her curds and whey;
Along came a spider, who sat down beside her,
And frightened Miss Muffit away.

JACK AND JILL

Jack and Jill went up the hill
To fetch a pail of water.
Jack fell down, and broke his crown,
And Jill came tumbling after.

TALLY-HO!

Tally-Ho! Tally-Ho!
A-hunting we will go!
We'll catch a fox,
And put him in a box,
And never let him go.

MIRROR, MIRROR

Mirror, mirror, tell me, am I pretty or plain?
Or am I downright ugly and ugly to remain?
Shall I marry a gentleman?
Shall I marry a clown?
Or shall I marry old Knives-and-Scissors,
Shouting through the town?

TWINKLE, TWINKLE, LITTLE STAR

Twinkle, twinkle, little star,
How I wonder what you are.
Up above the world so high,
Like a diamond in the sky.
Twinkle, twinkle, little star,
How I wonder what you are.

STAR LIGHT

Star light, star bright,
First star I see tonight,
I wish I may, I wish I might,
Have the wish I wish tonight.

THE MISCHIEVOUS RAVEN

A farmer went trotting upon his grey mare,
Bumpety, bumpety, bump!
With his daughter behind him so rosy and fair,
Lumpety, lumpety, lump!

A raven cried, "Croak!" and they all tumbled down,
Bumpety, bumpety, bump!
The mare broke her knees and the farmer his crown,
Lumpety, lumpety, lump!

The mischievous raven flew laughing away,
Bumpety, bumpety, bump!
And vowed he'd serve them the same the next day,
Lumpety, lumpety, lump!

DATE DUE

DATE DUE			
OCT. 05. 2001			

POSITIVELY
Mother Goose

DIANE LOOMANS · KAREN KOLBERG · JULIA LOOMANS
Illustrated by RONDA E. HENRICHSEN

H J Kramer Inc
Starseed Press
Tiburon, California

To the vision of a peaceful world
that lives in every child's heart.
D.L., K.K., J.L.

Dedicated with love
to Ryan, Garrett, Joshua, & Jacob
R.E.H.

THE BOLD WOMAN
WHO LIVED IN A SHOE

There was a bold woman
Who lived in a shoe.
She had many children,
And knew what to do.

"You are all lovable,
With special gifts," she said.
She hugged them all fondly
And tucked them in bed.

PART-OF-IT-ALL

There was an old woman called Part-of-It-All,
Who lived in a dwelling exceedingly small;
She stretched her mind to its utmost extent,
Then traveled through books to each continent.

THE KILKENNY CATS

There once were two cats of Kilkenny,
And with their friends they were many;
They'd wrestle a bit,
And then purring they'd sit,
Cleaning their nails
And licking their tails,
Until they all shined like a penny.

CHILDREN

What are children made of?
What are children made of?
Ships and sails
And heroic tales,
That's what children are made of.

What are children made of?
What are children made of?
Sweetness and spice
And gifts beyond price,
That's what children are made of.

LITTLE SALLY WATERS

Little Sally Waters, shining like the sun,
Thinking and dreaming of her future plans.
Rise, Sally, rise, open your eyes;
Fly to the east, fly to the west,
Fly to the dream that you love best.

IF

If all the seas were one sea,
What a great sea that would be!
If all the trees were one tree,
What a great tree that would be!
And if all the minds were one mind,
What a great mind that would be!

And if all the hearts were one heart,
What a great heart that would be!
And if the great heart took the great mind,
To save the great tree,
And clean the great sea,
What a great world it would be!

COCK-A-DOODLE-DO!

Cock-a-doodle-do!
I can tie my shoe,
While fiddling with a fiddlestick—
What a funny thing to do.

Cock-a-doodle-do!
You can be clever, too.
Just find yourself a fiddlestick,
And see what you can do.

HEY, DIDDLE, DIDDLE
Hey, diddle, diddle,
The cat and the fiddle,
The cow jumped over the moon;
The little dog laughed
To see such a sport,
And the dish said, "We'll all do it soon."

GOOSEY, GOOSEY, GANDER

Goosey, goosey, gander,
  Where shall I wander?
Upstairs and downstairs
  And in my inner chamber.

There I met a wise man
  Who liked to say his prayers;
He took me by the left hand
  And guided me with care.

MARY, MARY, EXTRAORDINARY

Mary, Mary, extraordinary,
How does your garden grow?
"Good thoughts are the power
That makes my mind flower;
Good deeds are the seeds that I sow."

SING A SONG OF SIXPENCE

Sing a song of sixpence,
A pocket full of sky;
Four-and-twenty blackbirds
Learning how to fly.

Early in the morning,
The birds began to sing;
Wasn't that a special way
Of waking up the king?

The king was in the counting house,
Giving gifts of money;
The queen was in the parlor,
Sharing bread and honey.

The maid was in the garden,
Hanging out the clothes,
When down came a blackbird
And kissed her on the nose.

SULKY SUE

Here's Sulky Sue, what shall we do?
Kiss her face, give her an embrace,
And wait till she comes to.

PETER, PETER, PUMPKIN EATER

Peter, Peter, pumpkin eater,
Had a wife who was a leader;
In a pumpkin they did dwell
And loved each other very well.

LITTLE MISS MUFFIT
Little Miss Muffit sat on a tuffet,
Eating her curds and whey;
Along came a spider, who sat down beside her,
And brightened Miss Muffit's whole day.

JACK AND JILL

Jack and Jill went up the hill
To fetch a pail of water.
Jack fell down, but didn't frown,
And Jill came laughing after.

TALLY-HO!

Tally-Ho! Tally-Ho!
On a nature hike we'll go!
We'll watch a fox,
And hunt for rocks,
And hear the river flow.

MIRROR, MIRROR

Mirror, mirror, tell me, how do I obtain
Beauty on the inside, the kind that will remain?
Become a gentle person,
And carefree as a clown,
Show happiness to all I meet
And spread it through the town?

TWINKLE, TWINKLE, LITTLE STAR
Twinkle, twinkle, little star,
How I wonder what you are.
Up above the world so high,
Like a diamond in the sky.
Twinkle, twinkle, little star,
How I wonder what you are.

STAR LIGHT
Star light, star bright,
First star I see tonight,
I believe with all my might,
I'll have the wish I wish tonight.

THE MAGNANIMOUS RAVEN

A farmer went trotting upon his grey mare,
Bumpety, bumpety, bump!
With his daughter behind him they went everywhere,
Lumpety, lumpety, lump!

A raven cried, "Croak! Beware gentlefolk,"
Bumpety, bumpety, bump!
"On the road up ahead there's fire and smoke,"
Lumpety, lumpety, lump!

The magnanimous raven flew humbly away,
Bumpety, bumpety, bump!
And vowed he'd serve them the same the next day,
Lumpety, lumpety, lump!

HUMPTY DUMPTY

Humpty Dumpty sat on a wall,
Humpty Dumpty had a great fall;
All the king's horses and all the king's men
Helped to put Humpty together again.

SOLOMON GRUNDY

Solomon Grundy, born on a Monday,
Looked on Tuesday, listened on Wednesday,
Learned on Thursday, loved on Friday,
Laughed on Saturday, leaped on Sunday.
This is the start of Solomon Grundy.

COFFEE AND TEA

Molly, my sister, and I spoke out,
"Being ourselves is what it's about."
She loved coffee, and I loved tea,
We didn't agree, but she still loved me.

ROCK-A-BYE, BABY

Rock-a-bye, baby, on the tree top;
When the wind blows, the cradle will rock;
Birdies and squirrels will be at play,
And you can watch them
All through the day.

SNUGGLY BABIES

Snuggly babies
Make happy ladies.

TOM, TOM, THE PIPER'S SON

Tom, Tom, the piper's son,
Invited a pig to go on a run.
The pig said, "Neat," and jumped to his feet,
And hand and hoof they ran down the street.

BIRDS OF A FEATHER
Birds of a feather flock together,
And so will pigs and swine;
Those who make the wisest choice,
Say, "All are friends of mine."

POLLY FLINDERS

Little Polly Flinders,
Sat beside the cinders,
Warming up each little toe;
Her mother came and sought her,
And joined her little daughter
To cuddle in the fire's glow.

THIS LITTLE MAN LIVED ALL ALONE

This little man lived all alone,
He was a man without sorrow;
For he believed in the world today,
And worked for a better tomorrow.

BED-HUGS
Good night, sleep tight,
A big hug and a kiss good night!

Text Copyright © 1991 by Diane Loomans, Karen Kolberg, and Julia Loomans
Illustrations Copyright ©1991 by Ronda E. Henrichsen

H J Kramer Inc
P. O. Box 1082
Tiburon, CA 94920

Art Director: Linda Kramer
Composition: Metrotype & Communication Arts
Book Production: Schuettge & Carleton
Printed in Hong Kong
10 9 8 7 6 5 4 3 2

Library of Congress Cataloging in Publication Data
Loomans, Diane, 1955—
    Positively Mother Goose / Diane Loomans, Julia Loomans, Karen Kolberg;
illustrated by Ronda E. Henrichsen.
        p.   cm.
    Summary: A collection of traditional nursery rhymes rewritten to emphasize
positive values and attitudes.
    ISBN 0-915811-24-3: $14.95
    1. Mother Goose—Parodies, imitations, etc.   2. Children's poetry, American.
3. Nursery rhymes, American.   [1. Nursery rhymes. 2. American poetry.]
I. Loomans, Julia, 1977—   . II. Kolberg, Karen, 1954—   III. Henrichsen, Ronda, ill.
IV. Mother Goose. Selections. V. Title.
PS3562.058P67   1991   90-52634
811' .54—dc20   CIP
                                                                       AC

HUMPTY DUMPTY

Humpty Dumpty sat on a wall,
Humpty Dumpty had a great fall;
All the king's horses and all the king's men
Couldn't put Humpty together again.

SOLOMON GRUNDY

Solomon Grundy, born on a Monday,
Christened on Tuesday, married on Wednesday,
Took ill on Thursday, worse on Friday,
Died on Saturday, buried on Sunday.
This is the end of Solomon Grundy.

COFFEE AND TEA

Molly, my sister, and I fell out,
And what do you think it was all about?
She loved coffee and I loved tea,
And that was the reason we couldn't agree.

ROCK-A-BYE, BABY

Rock-a-bye, baby, on the tree top;
When the wind blows, the cradle will rock;
When the bough breaks, the cradle will fall;
Down will come baby,
Cradle and all.

UGLY BABIES

Ugly babies
Make pretty ladies.

TOM, TOM, THE PIPER'S SON

Tom, Tom, the piper's son,
Stole a pig, and away he run.
The pig was eat, and Tom was beat,
And Tom ran crying down the street.

BIRDS OF A FEATHER

Birds of a feather flock together,
And so will pigs and swine;
Rats and mice will have their choice,
And so will I have mine.

POLLY FLINDERS

Little Polly Flinders,
Sat among the cinders,
Warming her pretty little toes;
Her mother came and caught her,
And spanked her little daughter
For spoiling her nice new clothes.

THIS LITTLE MAN LIVED ALL ALONE

This little man lived all alone,
And he was a man of sorrow;
For, if the weather was fair today,
He was sure it would rain tomorrow.

BEDBUGS

Good night, sleep tight,
Don't let the bedbugs bite.